CHERISH

A SCI-FI ALIEN BABY HOLIDAY SHORT

BARBARIANS OF THE SAND PLANET
BOOK SEVEN

TANA STONE

BROADMOOR BOOKS

For my amazing readers.
Wishing you all the happiest of holidays!

CHAPTER 1

*T*ori strode onto the bridge, glanced at the captain standing at one of the consoles, and released a sigh. "You should be sitting."

Danica swung her head around, pushing her blonde hair off her face and grinning. "You sound like K'alvek."

She crossed to the captain's chair that was positioned to overlook the half-moon shaped bridge and the wide view screen that showed the black expanse of space stretched out before them. Sinking into the high-backed ebony chair, she emitted a breathy groan.

"I sound nothing like your baby daddy," Tori said, " but the Dothvek does have a point—occasionally."

Danica rubbed a hand over her swollen belly and gave it a tender look before stealing a glance at her security chief. "Don't worry. I won't tell him you said that."

Tori fought the quirking of her lips, instead furrowing her already ridged brow. "Please don't." She scanned the readouts and found nothing anomalous, scowling again that there were no incoming ships or strange phenomenon. "Where is he anyway? I rarely see the two of you apart anymore."

1

She tried to keep the bitterness from her voice, but the words still sounded petulant to her own ears. It wasn't like she didn't have a right to be irritated. She and Danica used to be the ones who did everything together.

She'd been the first officer to join the crew when Danica had had nothing but the old, battered cruiser she'd inherited from her bounty hunter father and more guts than she deserved. Together, they'd built the crew up to become the galaxy's only all-female bounty hunting team and one of the most successful bounty hunting crews. Period.

Tori might not have been thrilled by the nickname they'd picked up along the way, but in her Zevrian heart, she would always be a bounty hunter babe—even if their crew did consist of as many males as females now, half of them from the barbarian planet onto which they'd been marooned and had finally escaped.

"He's still sleeping," Danica said, glancing back at the entrance to the bridge as if the gold skinned Dothvek might appear at any moment. "I slipped out without waking him."

"I thought pregnant women needed more sleep." Tori eyed Danica's tousled hair and the circles under her eyes. "Shouldn't you be resting?"

Danica bit her bottom lip. "I can't sleep much now. The baby is too big, and it's impossible to get comfortable. Besides, there's too much to do."

Tori swept her gaze across the empty bridge and the even emptier sky. It was fifth watch, so almost everyone onboard the ship would be sleeping, especially since Danica wasn't the only pregnant female on board. "Like what? Our last mission was with the Vandar, and although it was fun being a part of taking down the Zagrath Empire, it isn't like we've had much to do since then."

Danica worked her lower lip between her teeth. "I know

you're itching to bring in another bounty, but we have the holidays on the Dothvek home world."

"Human holidays," Tori reminded her. "Zevrians don't celebrate Christmas."

"Zevrians don't celebrate any holiday."

"Holidays are silly. This Christmas you insist on celebrating is all about putting presents around some pointy plant and then hoping a fat elf dressed in red shoves himself down a heating unit vent to fill up your socks with sugary foods."

Danica raised an eyebrow. "I guess when you look at it that way it seems strange."

Tori braced her arms wide on the console, baring her teeth, the pointy ones in the back flashing. "If an intruder attempts to board our ship through a heating vent, I promise you I won't wait to see if he intends to fill our footwear. He'll be put out an airlock."

"Poor Santa! Don't you like our tradition of exchanging presents?"

Tori shrugged, even though she had grown fond of their cobbled together Christmas parties where they drank too much spiced ale and exchanged presents they'd made for each other or sourced on their many bounty hunting missions. As much as she'd grumbled about celebrating Christmas before, she despised that everything would be different this year. "Do the Dothveks even care about Christmas?"

"I'm sure they will if we do." Danica gave Tori a side eye glance. "I know Vrax would do just about anything to make you happy."

Tori's cheeks warmed, and she grunted. Her mate would probably embrace Christmas wholeheartedly, the infuriating Dothvek. Even so, the thought of him made her heart beat faster. She gave her head a rough shake, focusing on her screen again. "I suppose Christmas isn't something I can keep from coming, but do we have to go back to the Dothvek home world for it? We just left that fiery ball of sand."

"It's been months." Danica put a hand to her belly. "Trust me on this. Besides, Christmas is about family, and I want our mates to see their families again."

Tori fought the nerves that jangled inside her. Family had never been her thing—except for the family she'd found with Danica and her crew—and the thought of visiting Vrax's kinsmen made her stomach tighten. There hadn't been much time between when they'd gotten together and when they'd left the planet, so she hadn't concerned herself with being scrutinized by his family. Then they'd been too busy in battle to think of much else, but going back for holidays meant lots of time doing nothing. And plenty of time for them to realize that she wasn't good enough for Vrax.

Tori cleared her throat. "It's a quick visit, right? Just Christmas, and we're gone?"

Danica didn't respond right away. "I wouldn't mind waiting a while."

Tori studied her friend's worried expression as her own fear grew. "What are we waiting for?" Then something occurred to her, and she gasped. "Do you want to wait until your baby is born or for all the babies to be born? We don't know when that will be because there's never been a Dothvek human baby born before."

Danica opened her mouth, but Tori held up a hand.

"Don't even try to say use Bexli's pregnancy as an example. She's a Lycithian shape shifter. Everything moves faster for her." Tori shuddered. "Plus, the baby wasn't even born normally. It shifted its way out."

Danica choked back a half laugh half sob. "I wish my baby would shift out."

Before Tori could press Danica, the doors swished open and they both jerked around. Instead of one of their female crew mates entering—or one of the burly, tattooed sand planet barbarians—a tiny green puff of fur raced inside.

Danica's shoulders relaxed, but Tori groaned. "Pog, what are you doing here? I thought we had a rule about no pets on the bridge."

"That's only your rule," Danica said.

Tori shot the Lycithian shape shifting *glurkin* a dark look. "I have nothing against Bexli's little friend aside from the fact that he leaves little turds all over the ship."

"If you don't like little turds, you're not going to be happy when all the babies arrive."

"Don't remind me," Tori grumbled, then froze as she stared at the little ball of fur scampering around the floor. "Hold on. How do we know this is Pog?"

Danica followed her gaze. "You don't think it's—?"

"Bexli's baby?" Tori nodded her head up and down, the metal sticks poking from her dark mass of curly hair bobbling. "I sure do. That little bugger loves to shift into Pog. I think it's the only thing he *can* shift into."

"That little bugger has a name, you know."

Tori flapped a hand impatiently at Danica. "That Lycithian-Dothvek combination she and Tommel came up with is too big for any child, and it's too complicated a name for me to remember."

"The rest of us call him Qek."

"Okay, Qek." Tori left her post and started following the little green puff. "Come here, Qekkie. You know you shouldn't be crawling around the ship on your own. Come to Auntie Tori."

Danica stifled a laugh, holding a hand over her mouth as her body shook. "Auntie Tori?"

"Not a word." Tori scooped up the green fur ball, cradling it in her arms as it wiggled wildly.

"Now this is a sight I never thought I'd see," Bexli said as she walked onto the bridge holding her sleeping baby in one arm. He had gold skin slightly paler than his father's, and pointed ears poked from thick black hair with the faintest hint of lavender at the tips. "Tori holding Pog."

Tori's mouth gaped as Danica burst into laughter, no longer hiding behind her hand. Tori looked at the sleeping infant, then down at Pog, then back at the baby. Before she could put him down, Pog dropped a perfectly round turd onto her shoe.

"Son of a *grunthik!*" Tori dropped Pog, who squealed and hurried toward Bexli, running behind her legs and cowering there.

Danica gasped for air. "No one is going to believe this."

Tori leveled a finger first at Danica and then at Bexli. "Because you're not going to tell them."

"Oh, I don't know." Bexli jiggled her baby as he made soft cooing noises. "This story might be what I give Caro as a Christmas present."

"What are you giving me?" the dark-haired pilot asked as she entered the bridge behind Bexli, then shook her head, her pony-tail swinging. "Never mind. Don't tell me. I don't want to know."

"What are you doing here?" Tori asked, glad for anything to distract from the fact that she'd been cuddling Pog and that she had a fresh turd on the top of her boot.

Caro took her position at one of the sitting consoles. "I set my alarm, so I'd be here in time to land us on the planet."

"What?" Tori spun around to see that the view out the front of the ship had changed. No longer was there only vast black space. In the distance was the unmistakable red sphere that was the Dothvek's desert planet.

She gulped, unleashing a string of Zevrian curses in her head. It was going to be a very sandy Christmas.

CHAPTER 2

K'alvek paused at the top of the metal ramp as it descended to the ground, sucking in the first lungful of dry, hot air from the planet. He might have adjusted to the climate controlled, purified environment on the ship, but it would never smell like home. The skin of his bare chest tingled as it warmed, and he let out a deep sigh when the bright light reflected off the golden sand reached his face.

"It is good to see the sands again." Kush came up to stand beside him, clapping a thick hand to his shoulder.

K'alvek tore his gaze away from the sand to look at his cousin and closest friend. "I didn't know how much I'd missed the feel of the suns."

"I know." It wasn't only that Kush felt the same way. Their people's empathic nature made it easy for him to sense this.

K'alvek nodded, glad that their powers had not faded since they'd left the planet. It had been an unspoken fear all the Dothveks had harbored since agreeing to join their mates as bounty hunters traveling through space.

Kush gave his kinsman's shoulder another firm thump. "Shall we go? I can smell the grilling meat from here."

TANA STONE

K'alvek's stomach rumbled at the mere suggestion of the meat that would be turning on a spit over the village's communal fire, drops of fat splattering onto the flames and sizzling hot onto the scorching coals.

Without turning, he sensed more of the Dothvek crew approaching behind them—Vrax, the youngest of their group and Tori's mate; Rukken, the former exile who was mated to Caro; and T'Kar, the Crestek who'd assimilated into their clan. The eager energy from all of them reverberated in K'alvek's own chest and racketed his anticipation until he could barely stop himself from barreling down the ramp.

"What are we waiting for?" Vrax gave a whoop as he bounded down the ramp then stopped, turning and using one muscular gold arm ringed in dark tribal tattoos to beckon them forward.

K'alvek and Kush exchanged a glance before striding down together, their footsteps quickening as they reached the bottom and their bare feet sank into the powdery sand.

Almost moaning from the feel of the hot sand cocooning his feet, K'alvek bent down and scooped a handful, letting the iridescent grains sift through his fingers before standing and wiping his hand on the front of his snug leather pants. His kinsman had all been swallowed up by the crowd of villagers who'd rushed out to meet them. All but Kush who remained by his side, as he always had.

The crowd parted as a pair of Dothvek females approached them, their long gowns fluttering in the arid desert breeze. Not only did both wear their dark hair piled on their heads in intricate braids and heavily line their dark eyes so they appeared upswept, but they both exuded regal power.

K'alvek dropped his head in a bow as the female in the golden robes that matched the sand in color and shimmer took his hands in hers. "Mother."

The female leader of the clan squeezed his hands, her love

8

and joy radiating into him as if it was his own. "It is good to see you, my son." She shifted her gaze to Kush, whom she'd raised alongside K'alvek, taking his hand as well. "And my other son."

Kush bent and kissed her hand. "Ruling suits you."

Kyrana let out a laugh that tinkled like the tiny bells edging the high peaked tents of the village oasis. "Always the charmer, Kush."

"One of us had to be," Kush said, elbowing his cousin.

K'alvek emitted a grunt that morphed into a reluctant laugh. He'd spent more time than he liked to admit angry and vengeful, but all that had changed once he'd met his mate and her bounty hunting crew.

The high priestess of the clan nodded to both warriors from behind the female ruler, her intense gaze moving over them before she smiled her approval. "Your arrival has been foretold and greatly anticipated. You bring blessings and prosperity with you, sons of Dothvek."

K'alvek and Kush both bowed to her reverently. They had grown up revering the goddesses who guided the planet and their people, and they could feel the balance these two ruling females had restored to the clan and the sands.

"We know it is not time for the festival of the suns," K'alvek said, "but we hope the village will help us celebrate the human holiday of Christmas."

The Dothvek's largest feast day occurred when the two suns that blazed above the planet grew closer and the days grew longer, and that wouldn't happen for many moons.

The high priestess exchanged a knowing smile with his mother. "If it is important to your mates, then it is important to us. We have been looking forward to this human celebration and preparing for your arrival."

He didn't ask how she'd known they would arrive. The high priestess had a connection with the planet's mother goddess energy that even he did not fully understand.

"Speaking of the human mates, where is my *senyata?*" His mother peered over his shoulder at the hulking gray ship perched on the sand.

Even though K'alvek and all the Dothveks had universal translators hooked to their ears to understand alien languages like the ones their mates spoke, it was comforting to hear his mother use the familiar form of the Dothvek word for daughter. Her choice of word made clear her affection for his mate. Despite being the reason her son had left the planet, Kyrana knew that Danica was also the reason for her son's happiness.

He didn't need to turn to sense Danica walking down the ramp behind him, but he turned to greet her, coiling a protective hand around her waist and placing another on her rounded belly.

The priestess cupped a hand over her mouth and let out an undulating wail that made his mate jump.

His mother pulled Danica toward her, kissing both cheeks. "Don't be alarmed. She is proclaiming the joy of our people at your impending birth."

Danica laughed nervously. "Not too impending I hope."

The priestess raised an eyebrow but K'alvek silenced her with a sharp look and a word of warning spoken directly to her mind.

"You must be eager for Dothvek food," his mother said, smoothing over the tense moment and distracting Danica by pulling her toward the village. "We've prepared a feast for your arrival."

K'alvek allowed his mother to lead his mate away, his heart constricting at the sight of his regal mother with her arm wrapped maternally around Danica.

"Sorry about that." Kush's mate, Max, was breathless as she hurried up to them. She flicked a hand through her short dark hair, pushing the side swept bangs behind one ear. "I wanted to bring some of my sample gathering equipment."

Kush made disapproving noises in the back of his throat. "I thought you agreed not to work during this holiday."

Max's cheeks flushed as she glanced at the leather satchel that was bursting at the seams with specimen jars. "Technically, it isn't Christmas yet. Besides, your home world has some amazing minerals. The sand alone has so many healing properties. If I could determine how—"

Before she could elaborate, Kush swept her up into a long kiss, curling an arm around her waist and lifting the petite female off the ground.

When he returned her to the earth and released her from the kiss, she gaped at him, her expression dazed. "I suppose I don't have to work the *entire* time."

Kush grinned at K'alvek as he led Max toward the village, ducking inside an open tent and closing the flaps.

"The matings seem to have been successful," the priestess said once Kush and Max had gone. "I sense nothing but contentment from your Dothvek brethren."

"The alien females might not be Dothvek, but they make good mates for us." K'alvek met the eyes of the high priestess.

"And the steel beast you fly in?"

He didn't glance back at the enormous vessel. "We have adjusted to life in space easier than I thought we would. Hunting bounties suits us, as does fighting with other species against unjust empires."

She inclined her head, searching his thoughts. "Freedom fighting has given you purpose, as has leading your Dothvek crew. You have always been a born leader, K'alvek."

He grunted at her compliment, fully aware that she would soon come upon the fears that had been plaguing him.

"Your father was also a born leader and a valiant ruler of our clan. Why do you think you will not live up to him?"

He lowered his voice as the sounds of merriment and

reunion rose from within the village. "Being a warrior comes naturally to me. I do not have any idea how to be a father."

"Especially not to a child who is of two worlds, human and Dothvek," she finished for him.

"I know I will love the child, but I do not know if I can teach him like my father taught me. There will be no sands to explore together and no communal fire to gather around and share clan stories and wisdom. How do I teach a Dothvek warrior to hunt on the sands and sense the rhythms of the planet if there is no planet?"

She touched her willowy fingers to his arm, giving him a curious smile. "Why do you think your child will be a male?"

K'alvek's pulse quickened, and his breath caught in his throat. A female child? A Dothvek girl? Now he was entirely out of his depth.

CHAPTER 3

*C*aro shaded her eyes with one hand as she walked off the ship with Holly by her side, who waddled more than walked down the ramp, one hand braced on her back. Both of their mates had gone ahead to the village, which had been fine with the women, who'd wanted to take their time leaving the ship.

"It's a little weird to be back here, isn't it?" Caro said, holding onto one of Holly's elbows to give her friend more balance—and so she wouldn't tip forward and roll down the ramp like a bowling ball. "Not bad weird but strange since the last time we landed here we were crash-landing and had no clue about the natives of the planet and now we're back with Dothvek mates and a bunch of babies on the way."

"Fuck, yeah it is." Holly blew out a breath and one of the red curls dangling over her forehead. "Let me tell you, when you're about a thousand weeks pregnant, a hot desert planet is not at the top of your wish list."

Caro swiped at the nape of her neck, already damp with sweat. "This will be a different kind of Christmas, that's for sure." It wasn't like she'd grown up with traditional celebrations, but she knew enough about the holiday to know that sand dunes and Bedouin-style tents weren't exactly fir trees and snow. She eyed the ship's engineer. "You're sure you want to stay in a tent?"

Holly nodded, her face set in determination as they reached the sand. "I might not be empathic, but I know T'Kar wants to spend time in the oasis village. He'd barely been assimilated as one of the clan when we left the planet. It's important to him to be near other Dothveks. Besides, everyone else is staying in a tent. I can hack it for a few nights."

Caro's heart tripped in her chest as she thought about staying in one of the large Dothvek tents. She had a lot of good memories from being in a tent with her mate, and her cheeks warmed at the thought of being back in the primitive dwellings. There was something exotic and sexy about sleeping in a tent as opposed to their sterile quarters on the ship.

"Last one there is a rotten *Preniki* egg!" Rynn barreled down the ramp behind them laughing and stealing glances over his shoulder.

Tori took long steps as she descended from the ship, the corner of her mouth quirking. "*Preniki* egg? Is that something you ate on Kurril?"

The boy Tori had rescued from the dangerous alien city shoved his sandy hair from his eyes. "Only if I managed to steal a lot of coin. They only last a day without going bad and then they smell like death."

Tori winked at Caro and Holly as she joined them at the bottom of the ramp. "Then let's hope you're faster than you look, kid."

"Kid?" Rynn put his hands on his hips. "I'm not a kid anymore. I'm a lot taller than I was when you met me."

Tori cocked her head, putting her hands on her own hips and making the chain belts around her waist jingle. "Which means you need to be fitted for new pants, kid."

14

Rynn wrinkled his nose. "New pants? Boring. How about a new blade?"

Tori laughed, grinning with unmistakable pride. "Negotiable. If you aren't the rotten *Preniki* egg." Then she bolted forward, sending the boy running after her, yelping with glee as they disappeared into the sea of tents that was the oasis village.

"For someone who claims not to be into kids or pets, Tori sure has taken to the kid." Holly rested a hand over the protruding belly that her colorful, floral-patterned top or her fluttery skirt didn't quite cover.

"Don't tell her I know, but apparently Tor was cuddling Pog earlier on the bridge."

"What?" Holly spluttered. "Tori can't stand Bexli's *glurkin*. He's always leaving turds on her bed."

Caro giggled. "For some reason Tori thought Pog was actually Qek, so she was holding him and calling herself Auntie Tori."

"Stop." Holly held up a hand as she laughed. "If I laugh any harder I might actually give birth right here on the sand."

"I take it you told her about Tori?"

Both women turned as Bexli walked down the ramp next to her mate Tommel who held their baby in one arm. His chest was emblazoned with intricate markings, which Qek traced with one chubby finger as he made cooing sounds at his father.

"It was too good to keep to myself," Caro said, wiping a tear of laughter from the corner of her eye.

"Did you tell her that Pog pooped on Tor's boot?" Tommel asked, his grin wide.

As if on cue, the little green puff of fur emerged from the ship and promptly rolled down the ramp, righting itself once it reached the sand and dashing off toward the village.

"I wish I could have been there." Holly gasped for air as she laughed.

"You were busy checking the engine one last time before we

engaged our landing thrusters," Caro squeezed her friend's arm, "which I appreciate."

Tommel inclined his head at Caro. "We all appreciated the gentle landing."

"I'm more than just a hot shot combat pilot," she said, "although I'm that too."

"Don't remind me about your combat flying." Holly shuddered. "I almost lost a fucking year off my life when we were helping the Vandar, and you barely escaped being blown up."

"I was never in real danger," Caro fluttered a hand at her friend, "but it is nice to take a break from flying for a while." She looked at Tommel. "You must be excited to come home and introduce everyone to your new son."

Tommel shifted the baby in his arm, using his free hand to rake through his dark hair, the silver glinting in the bright light from the two suns. "I never thought I would be a father."

Bexli leaned into him, beaming at him and her baby. "I guess you're lucky you got me knocked up so fast."

His eyes widened before his face split into a grin. "I guess I am."

Caro shook her head at the pair who were clearly besotted with each other. "You know you'll have to stop saying things like that once Qek can understand you." She pivoted to Holly. "And you're going to have to tone down all the cursing."

Holly's face fell. "Fuck me, you're right."

Caro sighed. "Maybe by the time Rukken and I have children, the ship will be a more suitable place."

"Or we'll have a bunch of kids running around who curse like Holly and fight like Tori," Bexli said with a shrug.

The pilot groaned. "That sounds terrifying."

"Are you coming?" Bexli twisted around as Tommel led her toward the village.

"Slowly," Caro said, cutting her gaze to Holly, "but you go ahead."

They walked behind Bexli and Tommel, falling farther behind until the couple had disappeared between the tents. When they'd reached the edge of the village, T'Kar appeared, his brow furrowed in worry as he looked at Holly.

"You should not have left the ship." He scooped her up into his arms as if she weighed nothing. "It's too hot for you out here."

"I'm fine," she insisted, but rested her head on his bare chest and the ornate design etched onto it. "Some water would be nice though."

T'Kar glanced at Caro but she waved him away. "Go. Get Holly some water. I'm going to look for Rukken."

He nodded gratefully, hurrying off to the glittering blue pond to one side of the village where tall palm-like trees swayed on the banks.

Caro tightened her ponytail and surveyed the village. It was much as she remembered it with a central fire where natives gathered around cooking meat, pens of braying and snuffling livestock, tethered *jebels* waiting for riders, and high-peaked tents stretching up into the blue sky. She didn't see her mate around the fire or the pond, so she headed for the tents.

Her boots sank into the sand as she wound through the maze of tents, some of them with flaps pulled back to reveal living spaces covered in woven rugs and some with flaps closed and soft urgent noises coming from within.

Before she could wonder if any of her crew mates were in those tents, an arm snaked around her waist, and she was yanked inside one.

"Do you remember the first time I claimed you inside a tent?" her mate whispered into her ear.

Caro's knees almost buckled as heat pulsed between her legs. Oh, she remembered.

CHAPTER 4

"I promised to help Danica with the holiday preparations," Holly protested as T'Kar carried her away from the bustling village and to the edge of the pond.

"There will be time for that," her mate set her gingerly beside the water and tugged off her shoes.

Unlike the rest of her crew, Holly rarely wore boots. Not only did they clash with almost all her cute outfits, but they were also murder now that her feet had started to swell. She let out an indecent sigh when T'Kar dipped her bare feet into the cool water.

"Screw Christmas." She braced her arms behind her and let her head fall back. "Just leave me here."

T'Kar chuckled, the deep sound rolling through her body and making her nipples harden. Fucking hell, everything made her horny lately.

Holly opened her eyes and peered around them. No one was nearby or watching, so she hitched her skirt up high and scooted down so more of her legs were in the water, closing her eyes again and letting the cool liquid caress her thighs. "That's better."

When she heard splashing next to her, she opened her eyes and saw that T'Kar had gone fully into the water. She was about to tell him that he'd ruin his leather pants when she spotted them in a pile next to her.

"Did you just strip down naked?" She glanced behind her again, but no one seemed to be paying attention to them, not that the Dothveks would blink twice at her mate dropping his pants. They weren't a modest people, nor did they care who heard them fucking in their tents.

"I wanted to swim." His gold skin glistened as he took long powerful strokes through the water.

Holly admired her mate's physique, trying not to think of her favorite parts below the water. Her heart was already beating faster and her nipples tingling as she watched him, and she was reminded just how she'd ended up so enormously pregnant. Part of her wanted to strip down and join him but the thought of doing anything more vigorous than sitting sent a wave of exhaustion through her.

A gentle breeze ruffled the fronds in the trees above her, and Holly dropped her head back again, letting her legs fall open. She needed some cooling off down there too.

Another splash—this one closer—made her open her eyes to find that T'Kar had swum up between her legs. He was almost entirely submerged in the water with only his shoulders and head rising above the surface. From behind her, or even to the side, no one would see him. Luckily, the opposite side of the pond—the only angle that would expose T'Kar—opened onto the sands and was devoid of watchful eyes.

She gave him a suspicious look. "What are you doing?"

He reached forward and grabbed her panties, tugging them down her legs and tossing them aside. "Helping you cool off."

She gasped as he slid his broad hands under her now-bare ass cheeks and pulled them into the water. The water lapped between her legs, sending desire prickling over her skin, and she groaned from the pleasure as she let her legs fall open wider. "I'm not sure if your plan is working."

T'Kar gave her a wicked grin, positioning himself between her thighs and parting her with his tongue. "Oh, it's working."

Holly bit her bottom lip as her mate dragged his tongue between her folds. She knew she should care that they were out in the open in broad daylight, but she didn't. She needed her mate to quench the fire that burned in her core and threatened to ignite her.

As his tongue swirled over her clit, she tipped her head to the suns and curled her hands into the long grasses along the bank. The cool water mixed with his hot tongue sent frissons of pleasure through her, the contrast of the two intoxicating. "Yes," she murmured, arching her hips.

Her body was so sensitive she nearly cried out when he slipped a thick finger inside her, but she pressed her lips together, only letting a whisper of a gasp escape.

T'Kar paused his tongue, whispering between her thighs. "Quiet, mate. Unless you want the village to know that my face is buried in your pussy."

"Maybe I do," she teased. The Dothveks had heard him fucking her in a tent before, and the thought had always excited her. Now the idea of them watching her mate spread her legs wide and lick her almost made her lightheaded with need.

"I don't mind the planet knowing how much I love to lick you, mate." He kissed the inside of her thigh. "There's nothing more delicious than your sweet pussy and feeling you come on my tongue."

That was supposed to keep her quiet? Her eyes rolled back in her head as she reached one hand around her belly and fisted it in his hair, holding him to her. "Then you'd better make me come fast, barbarian."

He let out a low growl, the sound buzzing against her skin and sending tremors through her entire body. Then he resumed licking her clit while stroking his finger in and out, curving it just enough to hit the perfect spot.

Within moments, her legs were trembling, and she panted as she tightened her grip on his hair. Waves of pleasure ripped through her, making her gasp as she threw her head back, her body spasming wildly. When she stopped trembling, she released his hair.

T'Kar sat up, wiping his mouth and grinning. "Like I said, delicious."

Holly's breathing was still ragged, but she pinned him with an intense gaze. "Now I need you to fuck me hard."

T'Kar's eyes widened. "This calls for a tent."

Holly licked her lower lip. "Does it?"

CHAPTER 5

"It's not exactly a Christmas tree." Danica eyed the palm tree that the twin warriors Trek and Dev had dragged into the communal area.

It wasn't one of the towering ones with curling blue bark that fringed the banks of the pond, and it looked nothing like the trees she'd seen in old images from Earth. Although she'd never managed to get a proper tree on board her ship, she'd had high hopes for the Dothvek home world. This tree, which barely reached her head, wasn't what she'd had in mind.

"We *are* in the middle of a desert." Tori shifted from one foot to the other as she scowled at the tree.

"We could always build a Christmas pyramid," Max suggested from where she sat on a nearby bench rifling through her bag. "That would fit in with the setting and be the right shape."

Danica gave the scientist a side eye glance. "We're not building a pyramid." She cocked her head at the tree with sparse fronds jutting from the trunk. "Once we decorate this, I'm sure it will be fine."

"How do you decorate a tree?" Tori scraped one hand

through her wild mane of curls as she twirled her pointy hair sticks in the other.

Danica walked closer and touched the droopy palm fronds. "Ideally, we'd drape garland and hang shiny balls from the branches," she touched the top and the cluster of fronds bursting up, "with a star at the top."

Tori cut her gaze to the two suns in the sky, both of which were sinking lower on the horizon. "A star?"

Danica laughed. "Not like a ball of fire and burning gas. Five points, usually in gold or silver."

"Humans," Tori muttered under her breath.

Trek and Dev, who'd been following the conversation back and forth, stifled smiles as they exchanged glances.

Danica ignored all of them, her gaze wandering to the tents that stretched out across the sands. Then she snapped her fingers. "Bells! We can use some of the tiny bells that edge the tent flaps. I'm sure there are extras somewhere, or we can pull the ones off mine and K'alvek's tent."

Max looked up, nodding. "Bells could be nice, especially if it's breezy. I've never seen a musical Christmas tree."

"Have you seen a real Christmas tree?" Danica asked her, her voice becoming almost reverent.

Max shrugged. "Sure. My mother loved all that vintage Earth stuff. Cheesy holiday music, lights, a big tree flocked with snow and covered with glass ornaments. It was one more way for her to impress people."

Danica didn't care so much about why Max had grown up celebrating Christmas, but she felt a pang of jealousy that the woman had experienced all that magic. "Was it the best time of the year?"

Max let out a breath. "I guess I didn't really appreciate it growing up. It was just one more thing my mother did that was over the top. Plus, she made me wear frilly dresses and Christmas pajamas that made me look like a giant candy cane."

Tori crinkled her nose. "This holiday sounds more and more bizarre."

Danica swallowed hard, wondering if her mother had been alive if she'd have been as into Christmas. Probably not, since even when she was alive they hadn't been rich, but it was nice to imagine cozy family Christmases not spent in a grimy spaceship alone with her dad and a sad present or two.

She waved a hand, also waving away the tears that threatened the backs of her eyelids. "It may not be perfect, but this is still going to be a great Christmas."

"Is this where we put the presents?" Bexli asked as she joined them. Instead of baby Qek, she carried an armful of small boxes tied with what looked like elaborately curled wire.

Danica beamed at her. "This is it. Right under the tree."

"Wait," Max said, jumping up. "You need something under the tree before the presents." She pivoted to Kush. "Is there a spare rug we could use?"

Kush grunted what sounded like a yes then grinned at his mate, walking past her and trailing one finger under her chin. "My little one always needs more supplies."

Max's cheeks flamed pink, calling after him. "This time it isn't for my experiments."

"I think it's sweet that he still calls you little one," Bexli said, winking at her friend, whose cheeks flushed even deeper.

Tori groaned. "It's a miracle I've survived the level of sweetness on our ship these days. I can only imagine how much worse it will be once all the babies arrive."

Bexli wagged one eyebrow at the Zevrian. "Lighten up, Auntie Tori."

Tori's mouth fell open as Max and Danica pressed hands over their mouths to keep from laughing. Luckily, Kush returned with a pair of colorful woven rugs that he wrapped around the base of the tree, and Bexli placed her boxes around it. They were further distracted when K'alvek walked up holding a string of bells.

"Kush said I was to take the bells from my tent?" He looked to Danica, his brow creased in confusion.

She clapped her hands and hurried to him, going up on tiptoes, throwing her arms around his neck, and giving him a hard kiss. "They're for the tree. Can you wrap them around it?"

K'alvek glanced at all the women with one slanted eyebrow lifted, as if asking if he'd heard right.

Max grinned, going up and taking them from the befuddled Dothvek. "Like this." She started at the bottom and wound them loosely on the uneven fronds. When she reached the point where she needed to stand on her toes, Kush came up behind her, cupping her body and plucking the bells from her outstretched hands. He finished the rest of the tree, making a mound of the remaining bells on the very top.

Several Dothveks had wandered over from the communal fire to observe the tree, but they appeared as confused as K'alvek.

"Since tonight is Christmas Eve, this when we drink my special spiced ale, right?" Tori asked. Her contribution to the shipboard holiday celebrations had always been to make the spiced drink they drank as they exchanged gifts.

Danica nodded, putting a hand to her belly and wincing for a beat. "That's right. I hope you have enough."

Tori swung her gaze around the village as bare-chested Dothveks milled about the pens tending to animals and emerged from the maze of tents. "I might need to make an extra batch."

K'alvek circled an arm around his mate's waist. "You're sure you are well enough to celebrate?"

"Of course." Danica gave him a look of mock severity. "I may not be able to get tipsy, but I'm not missing Christmas for anything."

He let his gaze drift to her belly as one eyebrow lifted in question.

"You're being paranoid, as usual. The baby isn't coming tonight." She was sure of it. The twinges were nothing new. She'd been having them off and on for a few days, and figured it was to be expected as she got closer. She pushed away the thoughts of the actual birth, fear fluttering like a desperate winged creature in her chest. "Trust me."

"Now that we have the tree sorted, shouldn't we plan the feast?" Max asked.

The other female bounty hunters gave her blank looks.

"Christmas dinner?" Max prodded, looking from face to face. "The big fancy feast? No?"

"My dad was never flush enough to pull off any type of feast," Danica said. "He'd get me some special candies, but dinner wasn't anything fancy."

Max held up her hands. "If we're going to introduce Christmas to the Dothveks, we're going to do it right." She pivoted to face Kush. "We're going to need some sort of roast meat. Whatever you serve at a victory banquet."

Kush looked to K'alvek. "We can take care of that."

Tori pulled her hair up and jabbed the sharp sticks into it. "I'll get to work on the spiced ale."

"You know what would be perfect?" Bexli twisted her head as she scanned the area. "Some of Caro's chocolate. I know she stocked up on our last supply run."

Danica rubbed her hands together, remembering the sweet treats their chocoholic pilot had baked for them before. "Where is Caro?"

CHAPTER 6

"*D*o you remember the first time I claimed you inside a tent?" Rukken asked, pulling Caro flush to him inside the tent. His heart thundered in his chest, his cock straining against the snug leather of his pants.

She gasped but didn't cry out as she arched her back. "What are you doing?"

The tent they'd occupied briefly before leaving the planet had been left empty, and it contained only a pile of rugs and leathers covering the undulating sand along with a tall center pole. Although it was daytime, the suns were setting and falling below the tent line, which meant the interior wasn't bright and sunny. Instead, shadows fell across the muted hues of the rugs. It wasn't exactly like the tent he'd had when he was exiled, but it would do.

The sight of his mate's beautiful, upturned eyes widening sent desire arrowing through him. As much as he loved being a part of the bounty hunting crew and flying across the galaxy fighting battles and capturing bounties, a part of him longed for the heat of the sands and a fabric roof over his head instead of a cold metal one.

Rukken pulled her so that she was facing the wooden pole in the center and lifted her arms high, tying them quickly with strips of fabric. "Taking full advantage of being in a tent again."

Caro twisted her face around, her pupils dark. "You don't need to tie me up anymore. I'm your mate now, not your captive."

He nuzzled his face in her neck, inhaling the sweet scent of her along with the smell of the sand and the roasting meat and the furry jebels. Closing his eyes, he let the blend of smells transport him to the tent in the middle of the sands when he'd captured Caro, stealing her from the village and claiming her as his mate. "Are you sure?"

She moaned, her throat vibrating against his lips. Rukken skimmed his hands down her lithe body, hooking his fingers in the waistband of her pants and tugging them until they'd cleared the curve of her hips.

"You wouldn't," she whispered, her voice a seductive tease and an echo of words she'd spoken to him before.

His body trembled as if he'd been electrified, a primitive need building up in his chest until he let out a velvety growl. "Wouldn't what, mate?"

She ground her bare ass into his aching cock. "Wouldn't fuck me while I'm tied up and helpless."

He almost laughed out loud. "You are far from helpless." Then he nipped at her earlobe. "But you are at my mercy, and at the mercy of my cock."

Rukken bent down, yanking her pants the rest of the way to the ground, tugging off her boots, and then pulling her pants all the way off. Caro emitted a startled yelp when he stood back up and parted her legs swiftly with one knee.

She craned her neck, glancing at the tent flap. "We aren't in the middle of the desert with no one to hear us anymore."

He wrapped one hand around her, slipping a finger between her hot folds and stroking her delicious bundle of nerves. "No, we're not. Anyone could hear me fucking you." He bent his head to buzz against her ear. "Unless you're very quiet."

She sucked in a breath as he moved his finger faster on her slick nub. "I'm starting to regret not killing you again."

Rukken used his free hand to grasp one of her hips and tilt her ass up. He tugged his leather pants down, freeing his cock and fisting it before sliding it through her wetness. "Your body disagrees with you. You're soaked for me."

"Because you never play fair."

He notched his thick crown at her entrance. "Once again, mate, I'm not playing." He drove himself deep with a single hard thrust, his eyes fluttering as her tight heat enveloped him. As much as they fucked on the ship, there was nothing like being inside her while she was tied up in his tent. The sight of her bending over with her hands wrapped to the pole fueled his barbarian desire to claim every part of the small female as his.

Caro bent her head back, her teeth biting into her lower lip to keep from screaming as he thrust into her again and again while working her wet nub.

Rukken moved the hand on her hip to her neck, holding it tightly. "Tell me again what you want. Do you want to kill me, or do you want me to keep fucking you?"

She attempted to twist her neck from his grasp, moaning as he buried his cock inside her. "I should want to kill you."

"But you don't, do you?"

She shook her head, rocking her hips into him to take him deeper.

"Say it, mate," he ordered, squeezing her neck slightly. "Tell me what you want."

"I want you to fuck me, Rukken," she whispered.

"How? How do you want it?"

Her eyelashes fluttered before they closed. "I want it hard. You know I like to take your huge cock hard and deep."

Rukken released her neck, gripping her hip again as her

body started to contract around him, her tight heat spasming as she bucked against him. He drove hard inside and held himself deep, savoring the feel of his mate's pleasure pulsing through her as she cried out. When her tremors slowed, he stroked into her one last time before throwing back his head and roaring as he filled her with his hot seed.

He sheathed his body over hers, raising his arms until his fingers intwined with hers on the pole. "There is still nothing so good as making you come on my cock."

"And you're still a cocky Dothvek."

He laughed, kissing the back of her neck and tasting the salty sweetness. "I'm *your* cocky Dothvek."

She moaned again, twitching her ass with his cock still snug inside her. "Yes, you are."

CHAPTER 7

*M*ax perched on Kush's lap as they sat around the crackling fire. The roast was rotating slowly on the metal spit—the flames dancing beneath it and making the skin golden brown—and the heat was warding off the chill of the desert night. She took a sip of her spiced ale and cuddled closer to the big Dothvek as he leaned forward to kiss her cheek, his long braid falling across his shoulder.

"Is this like a real Christmas?" he asked.

Max glanced around the Dothveks and bounty hunter babes sitting on wooden benches and standing with cups of cider in their hands. The tree jingled as the wind blew the fronds decked with bells, and the bottom was surrounded by roughly wrapped packages. Danica was trying to teach baby Qek to say "ho, ho, ho," but he mostly just gurgled and clapped his hands.

Max hadn't had a "real" Christmas since she'd lived with her parents, but even those holidays had felt too perfect and impersonal. This wasn't remotely as picture perfect as her mother's carefully curated Christmases, but there was so much more joy.

"It's perfect," she told Kush, twisting in his lap so she could wrap an arm around his shoulder. "The best Christmas I've ever had."

The clan's leader, Kyrana, sat in a high-backed wooden chair smiling and laughing with her son, who looked more relaxed than he had in days. Even the high priestess and her priestesses had joined the celebration and were sipping Tori's potent spiced ale. The twin warriors were slicing meat onto platters that were being passed around the group, and the occasional whoop went up among the crowd. Rynn was being instructed in holding a blade by Vrax, who continually threw his curved knife into the roasting beast, eliciting cheers from the young boy and eye rolls from Tori.

Initially, Tori had appeared uneasy when the Dothveks had greeted her warmly—especially Vrax's kinsmen—but the spiced ale she'd made seemed to have relaxed her as she stood with her mate's family. Max thought it was nice to see Tori smile, and not one of her teeth-baring grins that make enemies quiver.

"You mind if we steal her for a moment?" Holly said, appearing next to her and Kush and motioning for Max to follow her.

Max kissed her mate on the cheek and hopped up to follow the very pregnant woman. "Be right back."

Holly looped an arm through hers. "It's time for us to exchange bounty hunter babe presents. You're new to our little family, but we always exchange gifts between just us girls." She gave her a wicked grin. "What you and Kush give each other is none of our business although I'm not going to complain if you want to share the juicy details."

Max smiled. "Good. I've been working on my gifts for you all."

"You have?" Holly squeezed her arm.

"Danica mentioned the holiday exchange a while ago, so I knew it was coming."

The rest of the women had gathered to one side of the larger gathering, with a wooden bench pulled over and Danica already sitting in the middle, one hand bracing her back. She gave them a smile that was almost too bright.

"Now we're all here, we can start the gifting," the captain said. "Who wants to go first?"

Tori cleared her throat. "I usually go last because I've forgotten or have had to throw something together at the last minute, but this year I'm ready."

Bexli and Caro exchanged a look of surprise.

"All right, Tor," Danica said. "You're up."

Tori retrieved some lumpy packages from under the decorated palm tree, handing one to each of the babes. "All I have to say is this is Danica's fault."

Danica giggled as she ripped the brown paper, her mouth gaping as she pulled out the red fabric topped with a white puff of fur and cuffed with matched bands of white. "Where did you get Santa hats?"

Tori couldn't hide her smile or the flash of her pointy teeth. "Remember when we helped the Vandar on Carlogia? I had that little tailor make some for me."

Caro put on her hat, the pointy top flopping over to one side. "You had these custom made?"

Tori's brown cheeks looked slightly pink, although Max thought it might have been the heat of the fire.

"You know what this means, right?" Danica pulled her own hat on over her wavy blond hair. "You aren't a grinch after all, Tor."

Tori cocked her head at Danica. "A grinch? Is that an alien creature I've never heard of before?"

Danica laughed, cringing and holding her belly. "No. It's an Earth thing. But you are no longer one of them." She leveled a finger at the Zevrian. "You love Christmas."

"I love spiced ale and presents," Tori said from behind her cup as she took a large swig.

"Now that we're properly attired," Bexli said, her own Santa hat perched on her lavender bob, "it's my turn."

She scooped the boxes from under the tree and passed them out, practically bouncing on her toes with excitement. "These are a rarity from my home planet. I hope you like them."

Max unwound the wire bow and pulled the top off her box to reveal a clear faceted stone the color of Bexli's hair strung on a thin leather cord. She gasped when she realized what it was. "Lycithian crystal?"

Bexli nodded as all the women took out their crystal necklaces. "It's said to contain healing energy."

Max fingered the stone that was surprisingly warm to the touch. "It's also really rare with a crazy complex chemical compound. Scientists believe the crystal itself shifts according to the wearer's needs."

"They're fucking beautiful, Bex." Holly looped hers around her neck where it nestled in her cleavage.

"And your timing couldn't be better." Danica touched her fingers to the stone she'd hung around her neck. "I should probably go next." She picked up a pile of flat, oversized envelopes decorated with hand drawn swirls and passed it to Tori. "Take one and pass it, babes. I'm too fat to get up."

Tori snorted out a laugh, walking around the group and giving everyone an envelope.

Max opened hers carefully and peered inside, shaking out the single piece of thick paper. When she turned it around, she recognized the image that had been taken of the six of them at their first outpost stop after leaving the Dothvek home world.

They stood with arms wrapped around each other, laughing as K'alvek and Kush had tried to clumsily figure out how to work the device that would capture their image. Tori wore a crooked grin, clearly attempting not to laugh, while Holly's head was thrown back in total abandon. Bexli was turned and smiling at Danica with Pog tucked under her arm while Max and Caro were exchanging a bemused look.

"Danica," Caro said, her voice cracking. "This is amazing."

"It's us." Tori stared down at her picture. "All of us."

"I thought we needed a family picture." Danica beamed at them. "I know we're a bigger family now, and are about to get even bigger, but I wanted us to have a photo of the original crew."

"You included me," Max said, her throat thick with emotion.

Holly threw an arm around her. "You've been one of us since the day we accidentally nabbed you as a bounty."

"Absolutely," Bexli said while Caro bobbed her head up and down, dabbing at her eyes.

"I don't know how the rest of us are going to top all of this," Caro finally said through her tears.

"I hate to spoil the party, but do you mind if we postpone the rest of our exchange?" Danica's voice was high and breathy.

Tori swung her head to her friend. "Why?"

Danica managed a tight smile. "Because I'm in labor."

CHAPTER 8

"*W*ill you stop pacing?" Tori shot Caro a look as the pilot walked briskly back and forth in front of the tent within which Danica and K'alvek were having their baby.

Caro paused, wringing her hands. "I have to do something, and everyone always complains when I start to talk too much, but I can't just stand out here and do nothing, you know what I mean? Not when Danica is in there giving birth to the first Dothvek human baby. I mean, what if something goes wrong? What if humans can't give birth to Dothvek babies? The Dothveks are way bigger than us."

Tori held up her palms the second Caro's rapid-fire chatter stopped. "Never mind. Go back to pacing."

"Thank you." Caro resumed her small circle of steps.

"It's going to be fine," Bexli said, her lilting voice calm. "Danica is strong—and she's wearing her Lycithian healing crystal."

The crystals weren't magic, but they should make the birth process less painful for the captain. At least that was what Bexli hoped would happen. There wasn't much science around the mythical crystals. One thing she did know—they weren't making any of the other women less tense.

A loud moan came from inside the tent followed by some low voices.

"I don't know how these things work," Holly touched the lavender crystal around her neck and let out a nervous laugh, "but when I go into labor, I'm sticking it up my hoo-ha to take away the pain."

T'Kar's eyes widened as he stood behind her rubbing her shoulders.

"That's definitely not how it works," Bexli said as Tori rolled her eyes.

"We all need to take it down a few notches," the Zevrian's voice was sharp and commanding. "It's only childbirth. Females do this every day. It's completely natural."

Holly leveled a dark look at their security chief. "Talk to me when you have a Dothvek baby head coming out of you."

Tori reached for the cup that Vrax held as he approached her. "You're just in time." Then she drained it and handed it back to him.

Her mate cocked an eyebrow, glancing at Bexli. "Should I ask how it's going?"

"We haven't heard anything yet," Bexli told him, "but your mate could probably use some calming."

The Dothvek cut his eyes to Tori who'd taken the sharp metal sticks from her hair and was flicking them across the tops of her fingers. She still wore her Santa hat, but that didn't make her appear less menacing. "I'm not sure if that's possible."

Tori frowned at him. "I heard that, pretty boy."

Bexli shrugged at the Dothvek then grinned at Tommel who walked up behind her. She knew that being around the child-birth tent would be difficult for him since he'd lost his first mate while she'd been carrying their child. She reached for his hand and squeezed it. "You don't need to be here, my love."

"Qek is sleeping in our tent, and Pog is guarding the entrance, so I wanted to join you." He smiled at her, brushing a strand of hair from her eyes. "Since our son has been born, I only have good memories of childbirth."

"I'm glad." She squeezed his hand again. "Danica doesn't have the advantage of the baby being able to shift from her body though."

Tommel's jaw tightened. "The priestess will not let anything bad happen to her, nor will Kyrana. This is her first grandchild. They will summon the power of the goddesses to bring forth the child and guard the mother."

Bexli liked the sound of that and was reminded once again that her mate's planet revered females and their divine energy— a position she believed more cultures should take.

"We have brought food and ale." The twin warriors walked up with large wooden trays of savory meat and full cups of ale, the contents of the cups sloshing slightly as they walked. "We thought you might need sustenance."

"Now you're talking." Tori snatched a piece of meat from one of the trays. "Stress makes me hungry."

Once everyone had taken some meat and ale, the twins stepped close to Tommel.

"Could we speak with you?" Trek asked, his voice low as both warriors set their trays on the sand.

Tommel glanced at Bexli, who waved him away. The twins looked like they had something important to discuss. The identical, brawny Dothveks had always held a special place in her heart, especially since they'd been so gracious about Tommel chasing them away from her. She and Tommel hadn't officially been together, but he'd clearly wanted to stake his claim before the younger Dothveks made a move she might have been tempted to accept.

They are tempting, she thought to herself as her mate stepped to the side with them.

"Thank you for the meat and drink," Tommel said. "Your consideration is appreciated."

"We send only best wishes for K'alvek's child and mate." Dev bowed his head toward the tent.

"But this is not about that?"

It was clear from his expression that her mate already sensed what the twins wished to discuss.

Trek shook his head. "We wish to make formal amends for challenging you on the sands."

Bexli leaned back as she listened in to the conversation. She hadn't been aware the twins had challenged Tommel.

"I have long since forgotten that," Tommel replied. "You cannot be judged for finding my mate desirable."

So, it *had* been about her. Bexli found herself grinning even as she pretended not to be listening to their conversation.

"We do not want there to be any bad blood between us," Dev shifted from one foot to the other, "especially if we join your crew."

Tommel stilled. "You wish to join the bounty hunting crew?"

Both twins nodded, Trek adding, "We wish to travel the skies."

Tommel was quiet for a moment, and Bexli knew her mate was contemplating his response. "You are fine warriors, and any crew would be lucky to have you, but everyone on our ship— aside from the boy Rynn—is a mated pair. You should find mates before joining us or you will not be happy."

The young Dothvek warriors nodded grimly, no doubt sensing that his answer was intractable.

"Then we will find mates and join you." Dev bent his head abruptly and walked away, his brother following him.

Tommel released a long breath as he returned to her side.

"Everything okay?" she asked, feigning ignorance.

Her mate was clearly not fooled, but he curled his arms

around her from behind. "Better than okay, mate of my soul and mother of my child."

Before Bexli could sink fully into his embrace, the tent flaps few open and K'alvek stepped out, his expression radiant.

"The baby is born." His voice trembled with emotion. "A girl child."

Everyone cheered and whooped, Caro throwing herself at Tori, who wrapped her arms around the woman in a tight grip as they jumped up and down.

"Can we see them?" Max asked once the noise had simmered down.

K'avlek beckoned them inside. "Come."

They all entered the spacious tent that was in fact several tents connected to each other. At the far end of the complex of peaked structures, Danica sat up in a raised bed holding a tiny bundle in her arms.

"Come meet her," she said in a hushed voice as she looked up at her friends.

Everyone gathered around the bed, peering down at the tiny baby with skin that held the faintest shimmer of gold and a light brown tuft of hair on her head. The infant blinked up at the group with wide blue eyes.

"She's beautiful," Caro said, tearing up again.

"Does she have a name yet?" Holly rested a hand gently on Danica's leg under the blankets.

"Kylie." Danica touched a finger to her daughter's downy cheek then looked up at her friends with glistening eyes. "She's the best Christmas gift I could have imagined."

Tori took her Santa hat off her head and rested it gently on the baby's head. "You mean aside from the hats, right?"

Danica laughed as a tear rolled down her face. "Of course, aside from the hats."

Tori smiled at her friend, her own eyes shining.

Max put an arm around Bexli. "This really is the best Christmas I've ever had."

Bexli squeezed her and glanced over her shoulder at Tommel, who stood shoulder to shoulder with her friends' handsome Dothvek mates behind them. A sense of family and love—which were what the human holiday was supposed to be about—filled her completely. "It really is."

EPILOGUE

*T*he twin warriors stood at the edge of the village as the enormous ship lifted off the dunes, sending sand flying everywhere. They averted their eyes as the grains bit their skin and swirled around their legs.

Having their Dothvek kinsmen visit had been wonderful—they'd never had a Christmas before, and they'd liked the singing and the feasting—but it only served as a stark reminder that those warriors had found their mates and were starting families. Their lives were among the stars with the beautiful females, not on the sand planet with few females and little adventure.

"We should consider Kyrana's suggestion," Trek said once the gray hull was far enough above them that it disappeared from view.

Dev wrinkled his nose. "Crestek mates?"

"They're compatible, and many are desirable."

Dev scowled. He knew they'd forged a treaty with their former enemies, but it was hard to wipe away a lifetime of suspicion in a single agreement. Not only that, but the idea of living in the Crestek city was unthinkable, and he suspected a pampered Crestek female would find the oasis village to be primitive. But Tommel had made it very clear that he and his brother couldn't join the bounty hunting crew without mates. "What we need are females like the bounty hunters."

Trek shook his head impatiently. "There are no more female bounty hunters in the entire galaxy, and remember, we need two mates."

"We will be lucky to find one," Dev said under his breath, giving a final longing glance at the empty space the ship had occupied.

"One?" Trek scoffed.

Dev glanced at his twin brother but didn't say what they both knew. He didn't need to. Twins were rare among their kind, which meant they shared an even stronger empathic bond. It also meant that they could share their bond with a single female. Because it had been generations since there had been twin Dothveks, the tales of the last pair of warriors mated to one female seemed fantastical. The mated trio was only occasionally whispered about anymore, and neither twin knew if they believed such a thing, or it was truly a myth.

Myth or not, Dev and Trek had shared everything since they were boys, including their innermost thoughts. Would it be much different to share a female?

Dev looked up, realizing that his twin was easily reading his thoughts, his own brow furrowed. Before they could talk about it, something rumbled high above them.

Peering up into the almost white sky, Dev saw nothing until a spiral of smoke appeared almost like a wisp. Then the spiral continued to curl down and arch into the distance, leaving a trail of smoke behind it. They couldn't see where it finally disappeared, but it had landed somewhere in the middle of the sands.

Trek grasped his brother's arm. Without exchanging a word, they knew exactly what the other was thinking. The bounty hunter females had arrived on the planet in a burst of flame and smoke, crashing somewhere on the sands, where K'alvek had found them. Could they be so lucky?

The twin warriors took off running across the dunes, their hearts pounding and their legs pumping. They would soon find out.

* * *

THANK YOU FOR READING CHERISH! If you loved this story in the Barbarians of the Sand Planet series, you'll love the next book in the series, PRIZE.

Who do Trek and Dev find on the sands? Will their discovery finally fulfill their deepest darkest desires? Find out in the Barbarians of the Sand Planet novella, PRIZE, which will appear in the Science Fiction Romance Anthology, CLAIMED AMONG THE STARS. You can get the novella of Dev and Trek's story and the entire anthology (with 50 steamy sci-fi novellas) for only 99¢! The launch price is available for a limited time, so pre-order now!

Pre-order now: https://books2read.com/u/mB211y

* * *

This book has been edited and proofed, but typos are like little gremlins that like to sneak in when we're not looking. If you spot a typo, please report it to: tana@tanastone.com
Thank you!!

ALSO BY TANA STONE

The Barbarians of the Sand Planet Series:

BOUNTY (also available in AUDIO)

CAPTIVE (also available in AUDIO)

TORMENT (also available on AUDIO)

TRIBUTE (also available as AUDIO)

SAVAGE (also available in AUDIO)

CLAIM (also available on AUDIO)

CHERISH: A Holiday Baby Short (also available on AUDIO)

PRIZE

SECRET

RESCUE (appearing first in PETS IN SPACE #8)

Raider Warlords of the Vandar Series:

POSSESSED (also available in AUDIO)

PLUNDERED (also available in AUDIO)

PILLAGED (also available in AUDIO)

PURSUED (also available in AUDIO)

PUNISHED (also available on AUDIO)

PROVOKED (also available in AUDIO)

PRODIGAL

PRISONER

PROTECTOR

PRINCE

THE SKY CLAN OF THE TAORI:

SUBMIT (also available in AUDIO)

STALK (also available on AUDIO)

SEDUCE (also available on AUDIO)

SUBDUE

STORM

Inferno Force of the Drexian Warriors:

IGNITE (also available on AUDIO)

SCORCH (also available on AUDIO)

BURN (also available on AUDIO)

BLAZE (also available on AUDIO)

FLAME (also available on AUDIO)

COMBUST

The Tribute Brides of the Drexian Warriors Series:

TAMED (also available in AUDIO)

SEIZED (also available in AUDIO)

EXPOSED (also available in AUDIO)

RANSOMED (also available in AUDIO)

FORBIDDEN (also available in AUDIO)

BOUND (also available in AUDIO)

JINGLED (A Holiday Novella) (also in AUDIO)

CRAVED (also available in AUDIO)

STOLEN (also available in AUDIO)

SCARRED (also available in AUDIO)

ALIEN & MONSTER ONE-SHOTS:

ROGUE (also available in AUDIO)

VIXIN

SLIPPERY WHEN YETI

All the TANA STONE books available as audiobooks!

RAIDER WARLORDS OF THE VANDAR:

POSSESSED on AUDIBLE

PLUNDERED on AUDIBLE

PILLAGED on AUDIBLE

PURSUED on AUDIBLE

PUNISHED on AUDIBLE

PROVOKED on AUDIBLE

Alien Academy Series:

ROGUE on AUDIBLE

BARBARIANS OF THE SAND PLANET

BOUNTY on AUDIBLE

CAPTIVE on AUDIBLE

TORMENT on AUDIBLE

TRIBUTE on AUDIBLE

SAVAGE on AUDIBLE

CLAIM on AUDIBLE

TRIBUTE BRIDES OF THE DREXIAN WARRIORS

TAMED on AUDIBLE

SEIZED on AUDIBLE

EXPOSED on AUDIBLE

RANSOMED on AUDIBLE

FORBIDDEN on AUDIBLE

BOUND on AUDIBLE

JINGLED on AUDIBLE

CRAVED on AUDIBLE

STOLEN on AUDIBLE

SCARRED on AUDIBLE

INFERNO FORCE OF THE DREXIAN WARRIORS

IGNITE on AUDIBLE

ACKNOWLEDGMENTS

So many people go into a book's creation. My sincerest thanks to all the people who make it possible for me to create fun stories and share them with the world. Thank you to my cover designer, who is endlessly patient. Thank you to my editor, who catches so much. Thank you to my beta readers and typo hunters, who catch more of my goofs. Thank you to my review team for helping launch every book with lots of love. Thank you to my Facebook group for all the fun and laughs. And thank you to all the readers who read my books, write lovely reviews, follow me on TikTok or Instagram, and send me delightful emails. You make a solitary job feel not so solitary!

xoxo
Tana

ABOUT THE AUTHOR

Tana Stone is a bestselling sci-fi romance author who loves sexy aliens and independent heroines. Her favorite superhero is Thor (with Aquaman a close second because, well, Jason Momoa), her favorite dessert is key lime pie (okay, fine, *all* pie), and she loves Star Wars and Star Trek equally. She still laments the loss of *Firefly*.

She has one husband, two teenagers, and two neurotic cats. She sometimes wishes she could teleport to a holographic space station like the one in her tribute brides series (or maybe vacation at the oasis with the sand planet barbarians). :-)

She loves hearing from readers! Email her any questions or comments at tana@tanastone.com.

Want to hang out with Tana in her private Facebook group? Join on all the fun at: https://www.facebook.com/groups/tanastonestributes/